Frozen Mayhem

by

Jessica Bartos

DORRANCE
PUBLISHING CO
EST. 1920
PITTSBURGH, PENNSYLVANIA 15238

Dorrance Publishing Co
585 Alpha Drive
Suite 103
Pittsburgh, PA 15238
Visit our website at www.dorrancebookstore.com

ISBN: 978-1-6366-1189-1
eISBN: 978-1-6366-1779-4

Frozen Mayhem

Chapter 1

It lays at the bottom of the world. Its average temperature is negative 49 degrees Celsius and negative 56.2 degrees Fahrenheit. In the summer, around the coast the warmest temperature ever recorded was 15 degrees Celsius or 59 degrees Fahrenheit. That doesn't factor in the wind chill that makes Antarctica impossible to survive on. The longest journey lasted 105 days. The team was on the verge of death and had relied on half rations. They lost an average of 45 pounds each.

Saunders and L'Herpiniere made the journey on foot, dragging 400-pound sleds full of food and equipment. 105 days, that's a long time to be exposed to those temperatures. The average stay on Antarctica is 18 months. Some people stay less because in the winter most of the personnel go home. Only a few stays to keep the stations running through the long lonely winter months. I would have to say anyone was nuts for wanting to go there. But many people, especially tourists, go there. Mostly people go in the summer months to study animal life and see cute little penguins running around. Unfortunately, or fortunately, either way you see it, I am not a Biologist.

Another Scientist that's rarely seen on Antarctica is an Archaeologist. After all, the continent is covered in miles of ice. With only a few areas clear of ice and snow. Fortunately for me, I have a Major in Paleontology and only a Minor in Archaeology. Paleontologists are commonly invited down to the continent to try and predict past climates and Geological Fossils. Not that I would volunteer for that. Well, unless the money was right.

Dr. Charles Knoll sits at his desk examining a large chunk of fossilized bone. The bone is from a Mastodon, that was found buried in mud along the shores of the Great Lakes. It came from a Kill Site, from the bottom of a cliff along the rocky shore of Michigan. The fossil washed up on the beach and was found by a Grad student, then sent to Dr. Knoll to study. He stares down at the bone through a magnifying glass to see the grains in the bone. Since the bone is fossilized, he must dig into the middle of it to try and get DNA to test.

So, he picks up a drill with a coring bit and drills a small hole into the bone. After, he inserts a small needle and pulls out some material to test. Some of the material he sends out to try and extract DNA. The rest is used to Carbon Date the fossil. He sends the tests off, packs up the bone, and cleans his work station. After, he sits in his chair and ponders on Antarctica again.

Two miles of ice and snow. Wind speeds can reach 200 miles per hour. Making the Earth's 5th-Largest Continent a dangerous place. It has 750 miles of Gamburtsev Mountains, a range that is the biggest in the world. Reaching 9000 feet high. Many of the peaks are so slender that they are ice and snow free. The Continent also contains the Largest canyon, 6 miles wide and 62 miles long. There are also two active volcanoes. One of which never erupts above the ice surfaces.

Then, there is also the hidden lakes. Under all this ice there is more than 200 lakes. They're mostly fresh water so they don't freezer. Some Scientists believe that they are heated by lava vents that keeps the lakes from freezing under all that ice and snow. Lake Vostok is so warm, it is said to have a bubble of air or a dome melted into the ice up above it.

Antarctica, they are nuts asking me to go there. It's too long of trip and too far away from my work. Hell, the quarantine alone was two days. I would be stuck in a box house for two days, most likely with a boring Scientist. I chuckle as I think to myself, has my life come to this? Boring.... Boring.... Maybe I will go.

Dr. Charles Knoll sits up at his desk and picks up his cell phone. With a brief pause of hesitation, he hits the Government number on top of his phone registry. Another pause and a deep breath, he puts the phone up to his ear. One ring and then two....

A man answers in a gruff but polite voice. "Hello."

"Yes, this is Dr. Knoll."

"Yes?" the man asks with one word.

"Ahhhh, I'm in," Dr. Knoll says to the Government man on the phone.

"Excellent. There will be a car sent for you at your home in two days at 12:00 noon."

"Okay," says Dr. Knoll.

The man on the phone hangs up and Dr. Knoll presses the end button and puts his cell down on the desk.

"How does he know where I live?" he asks himself out loud. He shrugs and says, "The Government must know everything."

He goes back to leaning in his office chair. Ye. Boring....Boring being a Paleontologist. Especially when you can't get out in the field. He stares around the plain sterile workroom that he finds himself stuck in day after day, and looks at his self-made prison of drab work. He couldn't stand it if he didn't have the field to get out to once in a while. He looks at the only poster hanging on the wall. It says: "I want to believe." But instead of a UFO picture on it, there's a man killing and eating a dinosaur. Good spoof, he thought to himself, but it has meaning to him. Dr. Knoll is a believer in mankind's long existence on Earth.

"I'm not the only one," he says to himself.

Science has put back the date on early humans to over 40,000 years. Maybe even more. One human remain dug up in Israel was almost 200,000 years old. I don't think human remains can make it past that point, unless they are subjected to some very extreme preservation. Kind of like being frozen and trapped under the ice of Antarctica. Dr. Knoll nods off to sleep leaning back in his chair, dreaming of man's long existence.

Two days later Dr. Knoll peers over his printed copy of an email he received from the Government Agency involved in hiring him for this expedition. He packs all his warm weather clothes, including his Under Armor long underwear. The list says don't bother packing food. All will be provided. It says only essentials you can't live without. He pushed his clothes into his duffel bag. Plus lots of warm socks.

All my packing was done except for a big bottle of Luksusowa Potato vodka, that are sold all over the world markets. He pushed the vodka in his bag. He stops to make sure the bottle is in the middle of his clothes and thinks to himself, real vodka is not made out of grain but potatoes. He finishes closing his bag and sets it by the door. Next, he checks to see if he has his passport and other IDs in his travel bag. He closes it and sets it by the other bag. He sits down to wait until the vehicle arrives and picks him up.

He thinks of all the pros and cons of going to Antarctica again. Well, too late now, he already said yes. Let's see if they really know where I live. He thinks as he sits waiting for a knock on the door. The clock strikes noon time....knock knock knock. He opens the door and is greeted by a young Army Private in Military Uniform.

"Boy, you guys really believe in being punctual. Don't you?"

The Private says back, "Yes. Are you Dr. Knoll?"

"Yep, you got the right man," Dr. Knoll says as he helps the Private carry the bags out of the apartment.

The Private loads the bags into a black SUV with tinted windows and then opens the back door for Dr. Knoll. Inside the SUV were two back seats. So naturally being antisocial, Dr. Knoll sat in the very back seat. In the middle seat was a young, slim, blonde in a business suit. Next to her was a younger lady, possibly a native-looking lady wearing a University of California Berkley coat and stocking hat. He sat down and they introduced themselves.

"Hi, I'm Sylvia and this is Professor Louise Bryce from Berkley."

"Hello." He shook their hands from behind the seat. "I'm Dr. Knoll from Michigan State University. I'm a Paleontologist. What's your expertise?"

"I'm a historian. Louise here is a Professor of Archaeology."

"Do you know what this is all about?" Dr. Knoll asked the ladies.

The thirty-something blonde bombshell in the middle seat, closed up her phone and turned in her seat to say. "No, we were picked up at the airport here in Michigan, and told we were heading to Antarctica." She smiled at him with those beautiful red lips of hers. "They said there would be a delay in flights here in Michigan. So we'll have to catch a flight out tonight."

She turned to sit back straight in her seat as he asked. "Wait. Did you say Louise Bryce?"

"Yes," she said back to him.

"I read your paper in *Scientific America* about that Lost Mayan Pyramid on the West Coast."

"Yes, that was us."

"Well?"

"Well, what?" she asked.

"What happened? I heard there was a loss of life on that dig."

"You read the paper, didn't you?" she asked.

"Yes." he said back.

"That's all I can tell you," she answered. "The rest is classified."

"Hahh," he replied as he watched her turn around abruptly and put her hands together in her lap.

Sylvia leaned into her and took her clenched hands in hers and said, "Calm down and breathe."

Louise shook from the anger she was feeling. Dr. Knoll saw her shake and didn't press the matter further. He sat in silence the rest of the trip. He thought to himself, I wonder what really happened to those people that died. There must be more to the story. But he let it go and started writing in his field journal. Next, they stopped at another house and were met by another SUV that was picking up someone else.

Then in unison the two black SUVs headed to the private jet center in Chicago, Illinois. They reached the jet center at about 7 P.M. and were led to a private conference room. Now there was six people that were rounded up into the room. There was Dr. Charles Knoll in Paleontology; Professor Louise Bryce in Archaeology; Sylvia Cloud, a Historian; Aaron Maston, a Survival Specialist; Dr. Wade Emerit in Climatology; and Professor Karen Bradshaw in Geology. Out of all the Scientists, Dr. Knoll felt most comfortable around the Geologist. Because it was the closest Science to his own field. Karen was a good-looking brunette, which I guess didn't hurt either.

They all sat around a big table waiting for their presenter to arrive. An Army Intelligence Officer showed up with the Government Agent that tried to recruit Dr. Knoll earlier. The Army Officer was a spook, he could tell by his uniform. He only had a black patch where his unit patch was supposed to be. He had no name plate and no rank. The Government Agent was from the Office of Defence. Obviously a former military man, he followed orders to the letter. Each person at the table had a big blue binder in front of them.

"I'm Major Towns," the Government Agent said. "Open to page one of your booklet."

The Scientists all opened their booklets.

"Okay, you see the nondisclosure forms? No one will proceed without signing them first."

Louise read through the page and signed it. Dr. Knoll did the same and signed the bottom. One by one they all signed the nondisclosure form.

"Okay, good. Now turn to page 2. Lieutenant Groose will fill you in from here."

The Lieutenant stepped up in front of the table. He turned on a projector that was on the wall.

"Okay, this is what we know so far. A rift has formed in the ice over Lake Vostok. Under two miles of ice we have discovered a cavity several miles long and several miles wide that overshadows the Lake. We sent remote cameras down there to see if there was enough dry land around the Lake to send in a team to explore, and we saw this."

He flipped the pictures on the screen to a Lake shore free of ice.

"In a patch next to the Lake was green vegetation. It wasn't a very big patch, but it was a patch, nonetheless," the Lieutenant explained. "Then we saw this."

He switched the screen again. There was a picture of an old rock wall. A wall made of huge rocks with no visible mortar at the seams. It was just like other walls found on Easter Island and South America.

"As you can see," the Lieutenant explained, "this is a wall that should not exist on Antarctica. We have widened the rift to make it big enough to descend to the bottom and to explore this opening. You will be joined by several other explorers and Scientists at the site to explore and report back to the top. You will be leaving in an hour from this location and landing, after several stops, at McMurdo Station. You will then be flown by helo to the camp. Any questions?"

"What are you hoping to find down there?" Professor Bryce asked.

"We don't know yet, but I'm sure you will find that wall to be interesting. At least to start."

The briefing ended and the group was herded into the main department area. A huge C17 landed outside next to the building. The back of the plane opened up and a flight crew came out. The maintenance crew got to work refueling the plane. The group was introduced to the Captain, and then headed to their seats that were along the outside of the cargo bay. In the middle, there was snow cats and 9 pellets of equipment.

Lieutenant Groose was sitting with the pilots up in the cockpit for takeoff. Now if you have ever been on a C17 when it takes off, it's like being strapped to a very awkward rocket heading for space. It's not a smooth ride by any means. They went up almost vertical into the air. Everyone felt a little sick. Louise held her lunch pretty well, but Sylvia had to use the bag to get by. Dr. Knoll chucked a little bit as he looked around at the passengers' responses.

He was an Air Force Pilot back in his college days. He counted as the plane took off. One…two…three, that's how long it took Sylvia to pop. He was sitting next to her and handed her a bag. Louise's face almost turned green. Across from them was Karen Bradshaw, and she did pretty well through the whole thing. So did the other two men sitting next to her. Hell, the Survivalist, Aaron Maston, didn't even look up from the work he was doing on his tablet.

The plane stopped several times for fuel and the crew slept and ate on the plane. The whole trip was around 18 hours, according to the doctor's records, and everyone was exhausted. They were all huddled into personal sleeping huts upon arrival. These huts were connected at the center by a big commissary area. There's quarantine for the next two days, and Dr. Knoll sits at his table fighting off the sleep he just had. After the 18-hour trip he went right to sleep for 8 hours. But now he's up and waiting to find his composure to make it to breakfast.

"Ahh, hell, this jet leg isn't getting any better," he says as he heads out of his room and into the commons area.

The rest of the crew was already eating at the big table. He went to the chow line and dished up some eggs and bacon from the self-serve bar. He poured himself a glass of Orange juice and a glass of coffee. Grabbing a few sugar packets and some creamer, he headed towards the table.

"Look who finally woke up," said Wade Emmerit, the Climatologist.

He was a stout man, short in stature, and had a full beard. He looked like a lumberjack. Complete with his red, white, and black plaid shirt. Since he was being friendlier than the others, Dr. Knoll sat next to him.

He started to eat when Sylvia asked him, "So, Doctor, are you getting climatized?"

"Yes. I'm a little groggy but I'll manage."

Louise joined in by saying, "So we've been taking a tally on people's lives. So far everyone here is not married and most of us don't have commitments at this time." She winked at him.

Her smile was enticing to the doctor, especially when she wore that bright red lipstick.

"So I noticed that you're not wearing a ring, Doctor," Louise said.

"Yes, that is correct," Dr. Knoll said back.

"Do you have anyone waiting for you to, ahh…return?" Sylvia asked.

"No, I'm currently too busy for that sort of thing."

"Okay," Sylvia said, smiling. "We'll mark you down as single man."

They both giggled and went back to eating. Next, the Geologist approached him. At least she wasn't trolling for a husband.

"So, Dr. Knoll, what do you major in again?"

"Paleontology." he said to her.

"Dinosaurs? Or something more modern?"

"Much more modern." he said and took a sip of coffee. "I specialize in the Holecene area."

"Ahh. Mastodones and the like," she said.

"Yes, exactly. I knew I'd like you," he told her. "You know, I use a lot of Geology in every step of my work."

"Yes, I do know," she said with a cheeky smile.

She lifted her red-framed glasses up onto her nose. The doctor dazed off into her looks for a while. She had an off-color red lipstick and a beautiful smile that complemented her pure white face. Around her neck was a string of yarn holding up some kind of rock pendent. This woman is hot he thought to himself. Her waist was slim and she was tall. The only curves seen on her body was her medium-sized chest, that stuck out from her button-up white shirt.

"What kind of gem is that you're wearing?" he asked her.

"Oh, this," she said with a smile as she pulled it out from between her ample breasts. "It's a rose quartz from South Dakota."

"It's pretty," he told her and her smile got bigger.

He couldn't help but smile back. This beautiful, geeky, and professional woman was exactly his type. She stared at him a while as he ate. He saw her and stared back. They both swam in the fever of the moment until they were interrupted by Sylvia and Louise.

"So, Dr. Knoll. You're a Paleontologist?" Louise asked him.

"Yes, I am."

"Why do you think they need all of us with different fields under the ice?"

He stopped staring at Karen and looked at her. "I think they're covering all the bases," he answered.

He looked back at Karen to reconnect but she was talking to Dr. Emmerit. So he looked back at Louise and Sylvia with an "I'm taking the second-best route" look. Louise was a beautiful woman, but she seems a little childish for his taste. He liked his women more geeky, more outwardly intelligent. Though he thought Louise was professional and intelligent, he saw a college girl attitude in her.

Sylvia is a good-looking woman, but she is the typical thirty-year-old, still stuck in college girl. That type is fun but not something to commit to. A one night, maybe. Two nights tops, but no more than that. The conversation went on till the spook came into the room and sat down at one of the side tables, with the survival specialist. They were going over some information on the mission when Sylvia came up and sat down with them.

"So I hear you are a Survival Specialist, Aaron," Sylvia said to him.

"Yes, I am."

"Well, what does a survival specialist do?" she asked with a seductive smile.

"Well," he said, "they help civilians survive in extreme conditions like…the Arctic."

"Interesting," she said back. "Maybe you can teach me how to survive later."

"Sure." he said with a huge smile.

Chapter 2

 Quarantine sucks. Especially when you're surrounded by such a land to explore. Even if it might be dangerous out there, at least I'm not stuck in here. Most of the time I spend on the internet. Thank God for Wi-Fi. I can even work from here via computer and connect with my work desktop.

Just then, Dr. Knoll got a knock at the door. It was the spook, Lieutenant Groose.

"There will be a briefing in five minutes in the commons." he said and then left.

"Okay," I said back.

We all sat around the big table as the Survivalist briefed us on the cold temperatures.

"If outside, your skin must be covered at all times. Pay attention to the guide ropes and hook in at all times. Sudden winds can come out of nowhere and take you completely away. No one is to go outside alone."

Blaa...Blaa...Blaaa. The meeting went on. After the meeting was done, Dr. Knoll was heading back to his room when he was stopped by Louise.

"So I read your profile online and it says you minored in Archaeology."

"Yes, I did."

"Did you ever go out on a dig?"

"Yes. I went to Egypt in my third year."

"How long were you there?"

"One summer," he told her.

"Excellent," she said. "Can I count on you for help if I need it?"

"Sure. I do a lot of digging for my job anyway."

"Excellent," she said again. "See you later then."

He was like a kid in a candy store. He was being hit on by two girls at the same time. Maybe this Antarctica trip wasn't such a bad idea after all. When he got to his room Karen was there waiting for him.

"Some meeting, wasn't it?" she asked.

"Yes, if you like a hundred ways to die in the Arctic talk."

She laughed at his response. "Anyway, would you like to come over for a nightcap after supper tonight?" she asked with longing in her eyes.

"Sure." he said with a smile.

"Okay. I will see you at supper then," she said, smiling at him.

"You bet."

Damn, this trip was worth it. He returned to his work that he left in his room. He was really eager to get to supper.

Supper was hot dishes. All kinds of dishes and some of them looked pretty good. He filled his plate and in anticipation of eating with Karen, he took a seat at one of the side tables instead of the big table. He was hoping that he could talk to Karen alone. His plan worked and she sat opposite him.

Her hair was down and she was wearing contact lenses. Damn, he thought to himself, she looked good. The doctor looked away to the rest of the group. Sylvia was sitting with the survival specialist. Louise was sitting next to Wade and they were chatting it up like they've known each other for years. She laughed at something he said. She grabbed her necklace and put it in her mouth, a sure sign of hormonal acceptance. He thought to himself, they're going to get it on. He returned to looking at Karen. He tested her to see how close she was to liking his advances by complimenting her.

"Karen, I must say, you look beautiful tonight."

She laughed a little bit and then bit her lip. "Thank you."

Yep, definitely into him. They finished their supper and sat talking about their lives.

"I have some work to do out here for about half an hour." He pulled out his laptop. "Would you wait for me to have that nightcap?"

She smiled and said, "Your room or mine?"

"Ahh, yours."

"Okay. I'll meet you in half an hour." She headed off to her room.

After the doctor done with his work, he looked up to find that he was the only one left in the commissary. He packed up his stuff and headed back down the corridor towards Karen's room. As he was walking by the second room, the door was open and there was moaning coming out of the room. He snuck up and looked inside. The survival specialist was leaning back against the table moaning with Sylvia on her knees. She was moving closer and pulling back from Aaron as she sucked on his cock.

He moved quietly past the room and continued down the hall. The next door was open too and there was moaning coming from that room as well. He sneaked up to take a peek inside. There was Louise bent over her table with Wade pounding her from behind. He snuck past them and stopped. He thought to himself, what am I the only one not having sex right now? He shrugged his shoulders and then continued on to Karen's room. Her door was shut so he knocked.

"Come in," she called out.

He entered the room to find Karen dressed in a robe sitting on her bed. She was holding a bottle and two glasses. He sat down beside her and she poured him a drink. She sat cross-legged with her legs sticking out of her robe.

She drank a few sips and said, "Normally I don't engage in sexual encounters with men I barely know."

"Yes." he said back in agreement, staring at her naked thighs.

"But we are in Antarctica. I would like to experience this continent to its fullest. Do you mind if I use you to warm myself up for free love, while I'm here?"

The doctor was anticipating what was going to happen next. He reached over to touch her naked knee. She let him with a seductive smile and uncrossed her legs and directed his hand up her thigh.

"Of course I don't mind." he said as he reached her wet spot between her legs.

She leaned back as he fondled her button. Her dark hair slipped down from her shoulders and hit the bed as he held her up with one hand a few inches from the bed. The other hand was still stroking her clit. She moaned in delight as he played with her. She let the robe drop revealing her ample breasts. Dr. Knoll laid her down gently on the bed and moved his hand to her exposed breast. She shuttered as he played with her tit and pussy at the same time.

"More," she moaned in delight.

He moved his mouth to her other breast. He teased her tit and licked her nipple. He bit down on her nipple and she came with delight.

"Ohh. Take me," she cried out.

He didn't waste time removing his clothes and mounting her missionary style. He pushed her arms up and over her head and grabbed the edge of the bed. He pushed in her a little bit at a time until he was all the way in. Once he was in he started moving in and out as she screamed with delight.

"God....Oh, God, baby....Yes....Yesss." She came hard under him.

He wasn't done, so he turned her onto her stomach and mounted her from behind. He pushed his cock in and shoved it hard into her pussy. She was like a little Barbie doll under him. It was like he had his own personal sex doll lying under him. Only this doll was alive and enjoying every minute of his thrusts. He drove his dick hard into her waiting pussy and she cried out with every stroke.

"More...More....Oh, God...baby, more," Karen moaned out loud.

He took his time ramming her from behind. He reached under her and cupped her big boobs and squeezed them and came hard deep inside of her. She screamed at his explosion as she came too. He rolled off her so they were lying next to each other.

"That was wonderful," she said, breathing heavy as she took his hand.

They laid together spent for the moment. After an hour of laying silently together, Karen started to caress his inner thigh with her hand. He felt his cock become slightly hard as she slid up on top of his legs and bent over to suck on his half-hard cock. She stroked it with her hand and sucked it back to being fully erect. She slid up further on him and pushed his hard, throbbing cock into her waiting pussy. She rode him fast up and down then she switched her movements to front to back. She came again with his cock inside her. She turned around and he wondered for a bit what was happening, and then his cock felt hot, tight, and wet. She slid him into her tight butthole. She pushed down on him until she was sitting on his dick fully up her ass. She leaned back and laid down on top of him.

"You don't mind, do you?" she whispered to him.

"No." he said back, a little surprised.

"Good. Than pump into me," she said and put his hands on her breasts.

She pushed her ass down hard on his cock. There the doctor was laying on the bed with Karen laying with her back towards him, and he had his dick up her ass and his hands on her luscious big tits. He held tight to her tits and used them as handles to push his dick in and out of her ass. She moaned continuously as he jammed it home inside her tight hot ass. She was so tight and hot inside that it felt like his cock was on fire. He stroked in and out gently and then hard. She moaned louder as he came deep inside her butt. After they caught their breath, they went to take a shower and they washed each other off.

"That was wonderful," Doctor Knoll said as she washed his dick with soap and water.

She smiled and kissed him on the lips. "I thought you would like that."

Dr. Knoll had never experienced anal sex before and he was in awe at this new experience. Like a kid in a candy store, he asked, "Can we do that again?"

"Sure." She turned around in the very small shower stall.

She slightly bent over and spread her cheeks while he came up behind her and felt his way in. Instantly his cock felt hot as he pushed it in. Karen moaned excessively as he made it all the way to the hilt. He waited just a moment to savor the feel of her. He held her waist with both hands as he pushed into her hard. It was hard to move in the tight shower stall, but he had enough room to pump her ass with his cock. She moaned louder every time he buried his cock into her butt.

"More....Oh, more," she yelled.

They came loudly together. She turned around to kiss and wash him off again. They returned to the bed and laid down next to each other.

Chapter 3

 The next morning they woke up and said goodbye to each other. Karen made it very clear that she didn't want to get into a relationship while she was in Antarctica. The doctor, being a Scientist, ensured her it was okay and that he understood.

But he said with a smile as he left, "I would love to see you again while we are here."

"I can do that," Karen said back to him.

She blew him a kiss and went back into her room. Dr. Knoll proceeded to breakfast feeling good, he had just spent the night with a beautiful woman and he experienced anal sex with her. She didn't want to get tied down either. Okay, he thought, onto the blonde woman, Louise. What a trip. He sat down at one of the side tables to eat after getting his food. Sylvia and Louise sat down next to him.

"So, Doctor, I hear that you had a minor in Archaeology," Sylvia said with a smile.

Louise joined in. "He has been to Egypt as well."

"Sweet," Sylvia said. "Did you ever come across any naughty Egyptian graffiti in the tombs?"

"Yes. I saw the Senenmut Hatshepsut graffiti." He chuckled a little bit.

"What was that one about?" Sylvia asked him.

Louise smiled because she already knew the answer.

"Well, it depicts King Senenmmut taking Queen Hatshepsut from behind."

"Oh." Sylvia laughed a little bit, thinking it was a joke.

Dr. Knoll decided he was going to tease her a little bit so he said while looking at Louise, to see if she will play along, "Most scholars believe it depicts the first anal sex ever recorded."

Sylvia laughed so hard she almost fell out of her chair. Dr. Knoll waited for Louise, an actual Archeologist, to correct him and tell Sylvia the truth. But she just stared at him with a wicked smile on her face.

Just then Aaron came in the room and sat down at the big table.

"Excuse me," Sylvia said and took off to be by his side.

"Thank you for not telling on me," Dr. Knoll said to Louise.

"You're welcome," she said with a regular smile on her face.

"I hope I wasn't too gross for the poor girl."

"No. Sylvia is a very open girl," Louise explained. "She actually came over here with me to see if she could get a rise out of you. But you turned it on her pretty good. You know, I still haven't gotten you yet." Louise chuckled a little bit.

He picked up his coffee and started to sip it.

"I do teach a class on the eccentric practices of the ancient Egyptians. I could teach you a thing or two about that practice if you like," she said with a smirk.

Dr. Knoll choked on his coffee.

"Oh. Are you okay?" she asked him, smiling naughtily.

"Yes." he said, coughing and gasping for breath.

"Got you." She smiled really big at him and gave him a wink.

He grabbed her hand on the table and said, "So you did."

He squeezed her hand a couple of times in a friendly way and went back to drinking his coffee. She stared at him again with that naughty smile. He couldn't help it, he had to press this further, so he said, "That would be interesting."

She smiled at his response and said, "You know, I've been known to be open at times as well."

He choked on his coffee for the second time.

Louise laughed and said, "That stuff's dangerous."

"No, my dear. I think you are dangerous." he said with a sheepish smile. He grabbed her hand again and said, "Anytime."

She smiled big and told him, "I'll take that as a yes then." Louise stood up and went to join Sylvia at the big table.

Sometimes a man feels like he has been tricked and then sometimes he knows it. Dr. Knoll looked up to see Karen enter the room and get her food. She looked around to find Sylvia and Louise waving her over to sit with them. She did so to Dr. Knoll's bewilderment and they carried on a conversation like they had known each other for years. He thought to himself, what is she telling them?

They all laughed and Karen looked back at him and smiled. What the hell is going on here? Sylvia looked back at him and smiled. Then Louise did the same. They were talking about him, he knew it. He tried to ignore them and finish his breakfast. After a little while, Sylvia got up and came and sat down at his table again.

"Are you free tonight?" she asked as she smiled sexually at him.

"I guess I am." he said in bewilderment.

"How about around 8?" she asked.

"Well, I think I'm free," he answered.

"Good," she said as she got up and walked away.

Well, shit. He thought to himself. What did I get myself into now???

Sylvia returned to the big table and continued to talk to Louise and Karen. The doctor felt like a piece of meat hanging in the store.

Just then Wade sat down at his table with his food.

"You look perplexed," Wade said to him. "What's up?"

"What do you think of Louise and Sylvia?" he asked Wade.

"I think they are great. Why?"

"I think they have something planned for me tonight."

Wade laughed. "Whatever, it is just play along. Last night after I kissed Louise goodnight, I saw her and Sylvia meet in the hallway. Sylvia came to spend the night with me and Louise went to Aaron's room." Wade smiled big. "That was some night."

"Yeah, I bet it was," said Dr. Knoll, thinking of the possibilities.

The day did not go by so easy. At dinner the three girls sat together again. He could tell they were talking about him again.

Louise came over to his table and asked, "What's your favorite color?"

"Green."

She went back to the other table to talk with the other girls. They giggled and laughed as they glanced back at him. He ignored them as much as possible. At supper they all sat with him at the side table.

"Okay, what gives?" he asked as he watched them eat around him.

"Oh, nothing," Karen said as she continued to eat.

Louise and Sylvia just smiled and agreed with Karen. It was near 8 o'-clock when he finished eating and returned to his room. He walked in to find Karen sitting on his bed in a green nightie.

"Hi," she said as she sat there innocently.

"Hi," he said back.

He sat down next to her and she leaned over and started kissing him on the lips. Just then Sylvia strolled in wearing a green nightie as well and sat on the other side of him.

"So do you girls want a drink?" he asked them nervously.

He stood up and grabbed his bottle of Luksusowa. He reached for some glasses and poured them both a shot. Just then Louise walked in also wearing a green nightie.

Louise asked, "Do you have another one of those?"

"Yeah, sure," he said and reached for another glass.

She took it eagerly and he sat back down between Sylvia and Karen and took a drink. "So, ladies, what can I do for you?"

"Well," Louise said, "Karen was telling us how you have so much stamina. How you kept her occupied all night long."

He smiled a bit at that point.

Sylvia chimed in. "She said that you love all kinds of sexual positions." She stood up and Louise took her place on the bed.

"I figured," Karen spoke. "That we would see if you could keep up with the three of us."

They all put down their glasses and moved closer to him hungerly.

"Ahh, I'll try." he said as Karen started kissing him on the left side.

Louise started kissing and sucking on the right side of his neck. Sylvia opened his pants and headed for his well-endowed cock. She stroked it and when he least expected it she devoured his cock. She hit the floor with her knees and swallowed him whole. Louise and Karen helped him out of his shirt and started kissing his chest. Louise moved up to his mouth and started French kissing him. Karen moved down his chest and joined Sylvia on the floor. They took turns sucking on his cock until he couldn't stand it no more. Sylvia took her turn to swallow his come.

"Good job," Louise said with praise.

Karen moved up to kiss him again while Louise moved down to suck on his cock. She drew him in hard and sucked him strong. Meanwhile, Sylvia moved up and sat next to him on his right and put his hand between her legs. She laid down on the bed as he stroked her button. Louise gave up on sucking him and sat down on his wet cock. She hugged him hard as she rode him like a bull. She came hard. After she moved off him Karen jumped on and pushed him into laying down. She rode him as well moaning with delight. When she was done, Sylvia laid down next to him in the bed and pulled his cock to her waiting hole. He rode her from behind.

Louise laid down in front of Sylvia and put a strap-on dildo in her and gave the straps to Sylvia. Dr. Knoll graciously helped Sylvia strap it on. There they lay, Dr. Knoll fucking Sylvia from behind as Sylvia was fucking Louise from behind with the strap-on. Karen was joining in by fondling both the girls tits and his balls. Louise was moaning and Sylvia was groaning with Dr. Knoll being in heaven.

He had already came in Sylvia's mouth so he wasn't going to come anytime soon. The sight of these three girls having sex with him at the same time made him stay hard. When Louise was done coming, she got up and Karen took her place. She backed her pussy onto Sylvia's strap-on and instantly moaned. Sylvia came once and Dr. Knoll fucked her harder and she came a second time. Then Karen came right after Sylvia. Louise was fondling the doctor's balls as the two girls rolled away from him. The doctor rolled onto his back and Louise got on top of him and stroked his cock until he was rock hard. Then she sat up and guided his cock to her butt and sank down. Again he felt the heat and tightness of a girl's butt.

Louise looked down at his smile and said, "Karen told me you were very good at this."

She rode him back and forth as she pushed down to take his cock deeper. She moaned, "Ohhh, harder….deeper." Then she screamed out, "More, oh, yes, more."

Sylvia bent over the bed next to them and got on all fours as Karen put on the strap-on dildo. Karen slid the dildo into Sylvia's waiting ass. Sylvia moaned with delight as Karen fucked her ass. Louise watched this and couldn't help but come hard on the doctor's cock.

He was just about to come when Louise said, "Switch."

Everything stopped as the girls switched places. Sylvia got on the bed and the doctor slid up behind her and put his cock deep inside her butt-hole. Yep, still hot and still tight. Fuck, this is good, he thought as he pumped her ass. Next to him, Karen went on all fours as Louise put on the dildo. Louise got behind Karen and slowly pushed the dildo deep inside Karen's butt.

"Oh, yes," Karen moaned.

Sylvia was taking it hard as the doctor watched the other two girls going at it. She screamed out, "Fuck….Fuck….Yesss," and she came hard.

He came hard deep inside of Sylvia. He backed off a bit and they both watched as Louise fucked Karen. He couldn't help it, he got hard again.

22

Sylvia said loudly, "Girls, he's hard again."

"Come and fuck me," Louise said as she was still pounding Karen from behind. "Fuck my ass," she said as he got behind her.

He put his cock into Louise's ass. Sylvia came behind him and fondled his balls. She turned his head so that she could kiss him. He caught the view that they made in the mirror. There on the bed was Karen on all fours getting fucked with a dildo by Louise. Behind her the doctor was fucking Louise in the ass and loving it. Behind him was Sylvia fondling his balls and kissing his lips and neck.

"What a trip," he gasped out loud as he heard Karen come hard. He quickened his pace and Louise came next.

He still hadn't come when they split up so Karen jumped on top of him and put his cock into her slippery butthole. She was sitting so she faced him this time and rode him hard. She was done coming and she wanted to hear him come like last night. She quickened her pace as she drove his dick in deep. The other two girls helped as Louise took his balls and Sylvia put her tit into his mouth to suck.

They were all moaning when he shot his load loudly. "Ahhhh."

The girls got off of him and smiled at each other. Then Karen said, "See, I told you he came loudly for me."

"Yes, I heard it," Louise said.

Sylvia and Karen headed to the cramped shower and started to clean up. They soaped each other up and took turns washing off the soap. After they were done, they got back into their nighties and said goodnight and left together.

Louise sat next to Dr. Knoll and said, "Let's finish that drink." She handed the doctor his drink. "So, what do you think of my college buddies?"

"I thought I was being tricked," he said.

"Well, not really tricked," she told him. "More like shared."

"So, you know Karen then?"

"Yes. We all went to UCLA together our first four years of college." She finished her drink and said, "Let's go get cleaned up."

She grabbed his hand and led him to the shower. She washed his legs and chest. Then she moved to his cock and soaped it up.

"Oh, dear," she said as his dick got hard again. "What shall we do with this?"

The doctor was perplexed at this point. "I don't know."

She turned to face the wall of the shower and spread her butt cheeks. "I heard that you and Karen had a very good time in the shower this way."

"Yes," he moaned as he pushed his cock into her butthole.

He grabbed her waist, just as he did with Karen, and pushed his cock deep inside her ass. She moaned hard and didn't stop moaning as he pumped her ass in and out. There she stood up against the shower with her hands pressed against the shower wall, and she was slightly bent over and he was fucking her ass from behind. Damn, what a good trip this was. He came hard inside her. She washed him off again and they returned to the bed. She went over to the ice chest and poured another drink for them both. Then she filled an ice pack and threw it to him.

"What's this for?" he asked, and she motioned for him to put it on his balls and dick.

He did so as she sat down next to him and put on her nightie. She was satisfied and sat quietly next to him drinking.

"Thank you." he said when he realized the ice helped.

"You're welcome. Can I lay with you the rest of the night?"

"You most certainly may," he told her.

"Good, then you may need to ice."

She smiled and looked down at his crotch. His underwear was already starting to bulge.

"Let's give it a little rest," she said when she saw the semi-hard-on.

She reached over and kissed him and then returned to her drink. They sipped on the vodka for about an hour until they were both warm and toasty. She grabbed his empty glass on the nightstand and then walked over and flicked the lights off. She came back to bed and laid down and the doctor laid down behind her so they cuddled together. Her ass rubbed against his cock and he went up again. She pulled down her underwear and put his cock into her wet pussy. She moaned and they rode each other until they both came again and they fell asleep.

Chapter 4

The next morning the doctor woke up to find Louise gone. He was sore and had a hangover from last night. He rolled over in his bed and groaned. That was too much last night, he thought as he remembered every detail. His dick and balls were hurting so he got up long enough to fill his ice pack and get back to bed. He sat down and put his pillow behind his back and head. He heard a knock at the door so he covered up with his blanket.

"Yes?" he said and Sylvia came in.

"I brought you breakfast," she said and put a tray full of food in front of him.

"Oh, thank you." he said gratefully.

"We all thought you could use it after last night. Are you really sore?" Sylvia asked him.

"A little." he said and started to eat his food.

"I will leave you to it then," she said and then left.

She had a very wicked smile as she turned back at the door and blew him a kiss. After she left, he adjusted the ice pack on his crotch and groaned some more. Dr. Knoll stayed in bed that morning until at least 11 o'clock. Then he got dressed and headed out to the commons area to sit and work on his computer. He stayed there until dinner and ate. The three girls sat at the big table mostly silent. They would take turns glancing back at him and smiling.

Karen, after eating, came over to him and asked, "How are you feeling?"

"I'm a little sore but fine," he said.

"Good. I was worried about you," she said and put her hand on his shoulder. "We girls tend to wear a man out."

She smiled at him and he smiled back.

"Quarantine is done tonight so we will be moving to camp in a few hours. They have instructed us to pack and be ready to leave by 4 P.M."

"Okay, thanks. I will be ready," he said.

The Base Camp was big. It could house 100 people. Next to it was an old soviet camp that could house a few hundred more. The two groups did not mix. The Russians who occupied it did their own things as did the others. They headed out of the helo and into the main base entrance. There was two doors just like an air lock. This was to keep the base protected from all the wind and cold. Then, they were shown their rooms.

"Normally," Lieutenant Groose said, "this place would be filled with people. But this is the off season, so we are here with only staff and a few leftover Scientists. You will meet them later. To overcome confusion you will all have a complete tour of the place. This will reduce the chance of someone getting lost. Stow your gear and meet me down the hall in thirty." He walked in his room down the hall.

Dr. Knoll went into his room and put down his gear. When he came out he realized that he had a room between Karen and Louise. Ohh, boy, he thought, here comes more achy balls. He headed down the corridor to meet up with the rest of the group. Karen met him there and stood closely next to him.

"You see that we are neighbors?" she asked him, smiling a little.

"Yes, I did." he said with a smile too.

He thought back to that first time she put his cock into her ass and sat down on him. That ass...and then laid down on top of him and put his hands on her tits. Damn, that was a night to remember. He blushed the more he thought about it. She saw him blush and held his hand behind her back.

She squeezed his hand a few times and said, "Remember. We will do it again. I think I like you better one on one." She smiled and then reached up to kiss him on the cheek.

"Sounds good," he said.

Lieutenant Groose introduced them all to the engineer. "Mr. Causeway will take over now and give you a tour of the facility."

Then he left. Mr. Causeway gave us the grand tour. It lasted an hour. There was plenty of space on the base to move around and exercise. There was a full gym, a TV/movie room, a commons area, and plenty of places to get lost if you wanted to. They had many science labs open for people to use. In fact, it was a scientist's paradise. The whole base was up on stilts, two stories of housing, and all up on legs away from the cold of the barren ice below. The only thing touching the ground was the stairs and a few out buildings where they housed the equipment. One garage held a barrage of snow cats. That building was big and up on skis, so that it could be moved around as needed. Everything in this place was very thought out. Everything was made to survive this frozen wasteland.

Now if only I can survive the three nymphomaniacs, I'll be okay. I thought to myself, I need some fresh air. I asked Karen, "Would you like to come check the view with me?"

"Yes, I would," she agreed, and we headed down to the airlock to get dressed.

Karen was a little nervous as we stepped out the doors. I strapped her up to the cable and then strapped up myself. We walked together to the garage housing the snow cats and looked out into the ice-covered continent. It was beautiful. Cold and beautiful. We stared out at the miles of snow. It was romantic. She slipped on the way back and I caught her in my arms.

"Thank you," she said a little breathlessly.

We walked back and I took the buckle off the cable and took it to the building entrance. Then I did the same to mine. We entered the airlock and pressurized the first room. We went through the second door and got undressed. Karen looked at me with a new look on her face. I wasn't sure exactly what it was, but she had changed. She looked at me like I saved her life or something.

"Supper?" I asked as we headed to the commons area.

"Sure," she said as we strolled down the hallway.

"You know, I still have half a bottle of vodka left if you want to come by later."

"Are you up for it?" she asked me.

"I'll manage," I said as her face turned red. "How about you? Are you still sore?"

"A little bit," she answered.

"Well, we can be sore together if you like?"

"I would. How about around 9 o'clock then?" she asked me.

"Sounds good to me."

We headed to the food line. After supper, we headed towards the TV/movie room and sat down to watch *Whiteout*. Very fitting to be watching a movie about Antarctica while we were in Antarctica. She hung on my arm the whole time. Afterwards, I dropped her off at her room around 8:30 and headed to my own room to set things up. Karen came into my room and sat down on my bed. I came over and handed her a glass, before I could pour the vodka she pulled me down and kissed me. They laid down side by side kissing, touching, and rubbing each other.

She had changed, he thought. She didn't want just sex this time, she wanted to make love. He caressed her tits through her shirt and she rubbed his cock through his pants. He got hard and stayed that way. She stopped and pulled off her shirt and he played with her tits through her bra. She reached around and unsnapped her bra and let it fall off. Those boobs of hers fell into his waiting hands and he caressed them with his fingers. The nipples grew hard and erect. He laid her down on the bed and started kissing and sucking her breasts. At the same time he was humping her through her clothes. She cried in pleasured as he pushed his covered dick against her covered pussy.

She pushed him back so she could open and pull his pants down and he did the same to her pants. He slowly pushed his cock inside her inch by inch. She moaned with each with each inch that was pushed into her. After he was fully in, he pulled out slowly, and then pushed it all the way inside her pussy again. She gasped at his movement.

"Take me...oh, take me," she whispered.

He pushed his dick deep inside of her and laid his chest down on top of her. Her tits were like mounds under him as he started to hump her faster.

"Oh, fuck me...harder," she told him as he continued giving her his cock.

At first he went fast in and out, then he changed his tempo and moved slowly. She screamed at the pleasure of being teased this way.

"Ohhh. Yes...God," she cried over and over until she could not take it anymore.

She came and trembled as she laid there. He stopped for a moment to calm down a little bit, and then he slowly started up again. Slowly moving in and out of her pussy. This time she came even harder. He felt a tingle in his dick as he slammed it into her as far as he could, and it was time for him to come. Karen gasped out words as he was sliding his dick deep inside her wet pussy.

"Ahhh....Come, baby....Ohhh....Ohhh, come, baby."

They came together and collapsed into each other's arms.

The next morning the doctor woke up to find Karen had left him again during the night sometime. He got up to shower and shave and then head to breakfast. He sat alone at a side table eating when Lieutenant Groose came into the commons area and made an announcement.

"At 0900 we will be leaving for the entrance to the frozen lake. All available science crew will report to the airlock at this time. Bring whatever instruments and tools you need with you." He left the commons area right after.

Louise, Sylvia, and Karen were eating at a table together.

Sylvia asked Karen, "How was last night with the doctor?"

31

"It was fine," she said with a small smile on her face.

"Oh, come now. Tell us what happened," Louise said.

"Nothing special. We made out for a while and then we made love."

"What?" Sylvia asked in shock. "Love. What do you mean love?"

"Well, he was gentle, kind, and he slowly fucked me. We made love."

"That's it?" Louise asked.

"Yes. We made slow, good, and wholesome love," Karen answered her.

"That is the first time I have ever heard you call it love. Don't tell me you are falling for this man," Sylvia said.

"I don't know," Karen said. "Maybe I am a little."

"It's okay, honey. It happens to the best of us," Louise said.

Sylvia was furious. She slapped her fist upon the table. "We agreed that this trip we would all stay open, single, and not attached. Did we not? We even said we would share the men."

"Calm down, Sylvia. She can't help what she feels," Louise said calmly.

"Yes, but...."

Louise cut her off and said, "It's only natural, honey. We understand. You will have to live with it the rest of the trip if you decide to go down this road with him."

"I know. I'm so confused right now," Karen said and grabbed her head.

"Well, let's forget about it for now and get ready to see the site. Maybe you will think differently tomorrow."

"Yes, maybe you are right," Karen said back to Louise.

Sylvia huffed and puffed some more. Then she settled down after she thought about the people they had lost on the California Expedition.

Sylvia took a deep breath and said, "You're both right. If you are feeling this way you had better act on it before it is too late," she said to Louise and Karen.

They finished their food and headed to their rooms to get ready. They met in the airlock and found two new people who were going with them. Jason Adank is a biologist from Sweden and Agnet Baros (which is pronounced egg net) is a soil expert from Greece. Obviously, they didn't know anything more than the original team knew. Lieutenant Groose accompanied them everywhere.

The airlock was opened, and they strapped themselves to the cable outside the camp's main building. They made their way to the snow cat garage. Karen stayed right in front of Dr. Knoll. She was hoping he would have the opportunity to catch her again. That had been the turning point for her. She liked the doctor before that, but when he caught her outside the day before…she had feelings for him that went further than just fucking. She was looking to make him hers.

She slowly made her way in front of him as they walked along the cable. As they made it to the garage and the last few feet of cable, she wished he had caught her again. The crew was split up between four snow cats, which also had equipment in them. Drivers from the Navy were there to operate the cats and the equipment. Karen and Dr. Knoll rode together in one of the cats so they could chat with each other until they got to the site.

"Doctor, what do you think we will find down there?" Karen asked him.

"I don't know," he answered. "We know from the video that there is some kind of ecosystem down there and obviously some kind of ruins, hence the rock wall. So I think we will find evidence of past civilizations. But how old and how long ago did they exist, I can't tell you until we have more evidence."

"I think we will find geological evidence of advanced man's presence," Karen gave her opinion.

"Are you saying that you are a believer in ancient advanced societies?"

"A little," she said. "Something has to explain all the advanced objects and science found throughout the ages."

"I knew I liked you," he told her.

She smiled at his approval. Dr. Knoll was glad to see that Karen was taking a more closer approach to him. He really liked this girl and wanted to see more of her, perhaps even after this Antarctica adventure.

"So where do you live when you're not in Antarctica?" he asked her.

"I live in Duluth, Minnesota," she answered.

"That's only a couple hours from me." he said back to her.

He smiled at her and she smiled back. She thought in her head, probably at the same time as him, this could work!!!

Karen thought and asked, "Will you come visit me when this is all over?"

"Sure, absolutely." He smiled bigger and so did she.

They arrived at a big octahedron tent that was anchored in the ice and snow. The cats were stopped and directed into the big tent. Inside it was a balmy 60 degrees. They unpacked the gear and set it down on the ground. Then they went into an inner tent and waited for their briefing.

Lieutenant Groose started the meeting. "Okay, everyone. We will be reaching the bottom of these cable platforms. In a back-up situation, there will be tackle and rope with a harness already at the bottom. Everyone, just like on the top side, everyone will be in pairs of two. Do not stray farther than you can see the rest of the team."

"What? Wait...," Wade interrupted and asked, "How big is this cavern?"

"It's miles long," Groose said. "Vostok is as big as Lake Ontario. So DON'T get lost. The cavern is naturally lit by ice refraction, but there will be exterior lights set up as well. You will have flashlights and glow sticks for backup. As you are studying the area, we will be sending down a dive team to explore the Lake. So there will be a large light source at the water's edge at all times. Okay, you all have eight hours before we return to the surface. So good luck."

They all headed to the opening and the first team went down. Karen was standing next to Dr. Knoll when he noticed her put on a small necklace of some sort. The necklace was about 2"x3".

"What is that?" he asked.

"Oh, this. It's from Louise and Sylvia. They told me to wear it anytime I'm down in the ice."

"I'm pretty sure it's a radiation monitor," the doctor said.

"Well, that would make sense," she explained. "Some people died of radiation the last time they were in the field."

"Radiation in an Archeological dig? That must have been bad," the doctor said. He looked over at Sylvia and Louise, they were wearing the same devices too.

"I'm staying with you then," Dr. Knoll said to Karen.

"Fine with me," she said, smiling.

The four of them went down on the same lift and Sylvia said, "Here we go."

"I hope this is worth it," Louise said.

"I'm sure it will be, Professor," Dr. Knoll commented.

Karen just held her breath as they were surrounded by walls of ice. The tunnel going down was no wider than a foot around the lift. It took well over 20 minutes to reach the ground.

"All out," the Navy officer said as he opened the door. "Stand clear," he yelled as the lift went back up in the air.

They got out of the lift a hundred yards from the lake shore. By the lake they had set up big spotlights on a scaffolding. They were pointing out into an endless lake. Louise and Sylvia headed to those lights and Dr. Knoll and Karen were behind them.

"Beautiful," Louise said.

"What?" Karen asked from behind the two.

"Look." Sylvia pointed towards the lake.

The lights shone into the water that was pure sea blue. Not see-through but sea blue colored. It was a sight that none has ever seen. The doctor looked out into the never-ending blue lake. It was waveless, calm, and sea blue.

"Well, that is…."

Karen interrupted him, "Beautiful." She finished his sentence.

"Awe, how sweet," Sylvia said. "They are finishing each other's sentences now."

"Oh, shut up, Sylvia," Louise said.

Karen's face turned red. Louise and Sylvia went off down an old trail.

"It's okay," the doctor said. "I like you a lot too. I don't care if people know it."

She giggled and then kissed his cheek. They watched Louise and Sylvia walk off into the dim light.

"So where should we start?" Karen asked.

"Let's go find that wall," he said.

They went off towards a post lamp off in the distance. As they approached, Lieutenant Groose was already there talking to Louise and Sylvia. Louise was down on the ground next to the wall with some tools inspecting the stone work. Dr. Knoll kneeled down and looked at the structure. The wall was only a few feet tall, and the top looked like it had been worn away by glacial weathering. But the sides were untouched. So he started there.

After a few moments, he looked up at Karen and said, "Yep. It's definitely manmade. It's also advanced stonework."

"Yep," Louise added. "Just like South America and Easter Island. The stone is placed one on top of each other without mortar. No gaps like it had been melted into place. I always wondered about these structures. How do you think they built them?"

Dr. Knoll shook his head. "I don't know."

Karen being a Geologist pulled out a small hammer and hit the edge of the stone. A small chunk fell off and she started examining it under a small magnifying glass. She stared at it for a while looking at each side.

"Yes...yes, this is Andesite. One of the strongest rocks in the world. But something is wrong here. It looks like the rock has been melted and then re-hardened recently," Karen told the group.

"Recently? Like in the last year?" Sylvia asked.

"No," the doctor interrupted. "Recent in Geological terms means in the last 10-20 thousand years."

Karen nodded her head in agreement. "Precisely 10-15 thousand years ago."

"Well, that means Antarctica was ice free at that time," Louise said.

"Let's look farther down," Sylvia said.

They moved on down the lake shore. This time they came upon the Biologist and the soil expert kneeling down over a patch a green vegetation.

"Look at it," Jason Adank said in his Swedish accent.

"Yes. Get a sample of the soil, please," Agnet said.

"That's cotton plants," Jason said. "How in the hell did that get down here?" he asked with amazement in his voice.

"And there is clover," said Agnet, pointing.

Sylvia stood across from Jason as he bent down looking at the ground. He had white yellowish hair and blue eyes. He was very muscular and fit. He was wearing a t-shirt and jeans, and she swore she could see a big bulge in his pants.

"Hmmm," she hummed under her breath. "This guy is smoking hot."

On the other side, Louise was standing and checking out the soil expert. She had dark hair and green eyes. She was wearing coveralls but Louise could still make out her perfectly curved waist. Those breasts of hers popped out of the coveralls so they were only covered by a thin t-shirt. Louise couldn't get over her beauty.

"Tell me, Agnet, how do you think this vegetation got down here?"

"Well, I think the seeds went dormant in the soil when the continent got iced over. When they saw the opportunity to grow back, they took it."

"Is this soil fertile enough for that?" Dr. Knoll asked her.

"It is," Karen said. "Under a glacier all the nutrients in the ice mix with the soil and make a very good growing mix."

"Yes, I agree," Agnet said. "The soil would even be rich in nitrogen from the melting ice. Perfect growing dirt."

Just then Sylvia called out from the darkness, "Come quick and look at this."

They all ran to her side. There in front of them was a marker. It was made out of stone and there was writing on it.

"Do you see this?" Louise asked. "This is proto Egyptian. Here and here." She pointed at the engravings. "I need to study these."

She started rubbing a graphite stick across a piece of wax paper on the markers. She was making copies of them so she could study them later.

"There. I'm done," Louise said.

"Wait. Here is another one and another one," Sylvia said.

Sure enough, there was a small yard full of stone markers. There was a graveyard under the ice. The others followed the row of stones while Louise kept rubbing them. She finished each one and sat there for a moment and tried to read them. After her last encounter with proto Egyptian, she had learned the language. Well, some of it, anyway. She went back to rubbing the inscriptions on the stones until she ran out of wax paper. Then, she sat up against one of the stones and paged through the papers. This is so familiar. Here this one looks like Mayan, and here ancient Chinese. What is going on here?

Sylvia came back and Louise told her, "We need to start digging here."

"I'll get the Lieutenant," she said.

Sylvia ran off to the other group about a hundred yards up the shore.

Lieutenant asked as she came running up, "Where is your partner?"

"Ahh, she's right there," she said, pointing down the lake shore. "She needs to set up a dig site."

He walked back to the field of marked stones with her. "Professor, what do you have here?"

"I think it's a communal graveyard. If we can get some tissue for DNA testing, we can find out who these people were. We need to dig here," Louise said.

"Not today. We will be back tomorrow and you can dig then. Where did the rest of your group go?" the Lieutenant asked.

"They were just down there," Louise said.

Sylvia led them to the rest of the group she had been with. The Lieutenant, Louise, and Sylvia passed many stones as they made their way towards the other group. Dr. Knoll was kneeling by what looked like a statue. Karen was studying the makeup of its stone. Agnet and Jason were off to the left looking at something else. Karen started taking pictures of the small statue when the three approached.

"Interesting. That looks like African," Louise said.

"How many cultures are we going to find down here?" Sylvia asked.

"Remember the last dig?" Louise asked. "We found at least three. What if all these...."

They were interrupted by Agnet and Jason yelling for them to come over.

"What is it?" the doctor asked as he approached the site.

Silence took over the crowd.

"Eweee," shirked Sylvia.

"What is that smell?" Louise asked in disgust.

There in front of them was the head and tusks of a large mammoth. The skull had no flesh on it. Behind the head was the rotting flesh of its neck. Its body was still intact but flat, like it had been crushed by the weight of ice. Lots of ice. Agnet touched the back of the body and it was still frozen.

"Look," Agnet said. "The mud is preserving the cold. It's half buried in the permafrost."

"What is it doing here?" Jason asked.

"It's just like the mammoths in Siberia. It was flash frozen," the doctor said. "Where is Wade Emmerite?"

"He just arrived a little bit ago at the stone markers," the Lieutenant said. "I'll go get him."

He scooted away into the half-light. The team stayed there trying to study the creature. All except for Karen, she was looking at the mineral deposits in the surrounding dirt.

"Pays to be a Geologist," she said as she held her nose and studied the rocks far enough away to try and avoid the smell.

The mammoth tusks were tall, standing high over Jason's head.

"That's at least 16 feet," Dr. Knoll said in amazement.

Jason the Biologist agreed. This was a full-grown mammoth. Agnet was still looking at the back of the animal. Karen was off to the side trying not to throw up. Sylvia and Louise were going over the rubbing a few feet away. When all of a sudden the noise of a big crash filled the air. Wade, the survivalist, and the Lieutenant approached right behind the team. They asked them what they had heard.

"Stay here," the Lieutenant ordered and him and the survivalist took off in the direction of the noise.

The group continued to study the mammoth.

"What in the hell?" Wade asked.

He fell to his knees and studied the beast. This would mean that the hologean started with a flash freeze like some Climatologists have predicted. This could happen at any time. He was distraught.

"We need to warn people," Wade said.

"I don't know if they will let you do that," Louise said. "Remember, you signed a nondisclosure form. We did on our last dig and couldn't even tell the truth about how people died."

Sylvia nodded her head in agreement. "Yep, it was brutal not telling people what happened."

"Well, we'll just see about that," Wade said.

"I wouldn't," Dr. Knoll said. "They can put you in prison for the rest of your life if you do."

Dr. Knoll knew well enough being in the Air Force that they could. Karen returned to see what the commotion was. She heard the last of the conversation and stayed quiet. She knew what had happened at the dig in California and what Louise and Sylvia had went through. After a few minutes the Lieutenant came running up with the survivalist.

"We are leaving," he said. "Now."

The group was instructed to get back to the platform immediately. They were literally shown to the exit. When they got there, the divers from the lake were laying close to the platform. One of them was bandaging up the other two. Dr. Knoll looked towards the lake to see the big light structure was tipped over and half submerged in the lake.

"Can I help?" he asked, looking back at the injured Navy divers.

"Yes, put pressure here," the Navy Medic said.

Just then the platform thudded to the ground and seven Marines popped out of the door and surrounded the group with heavy machine guns. They loaded the group, this time as many as they could fit onto the platform and headed to the surface. They put eight in and hauled them to the top at a very fast speed. Sylvia threw up halfway up from the speed. The rest of the group came up 20 minutes later. Then the Marines were the last to come up. They sealed the hole with a heavy iron door and then placed the heavy lift on top of that.

"That's all for today, folks," the Lieutenant said. "Let's get you back to the base."

They all headed for the cats scratching their heads. They wondered what happened to the divers. Once they got back to base, the whole team sat at the main table trying to figure out what happened. Everyone had their own theories. The Survivalist came into the room and, after getting his food, sat down with the others.

"What did you see?" Sylvia asked him, curious about his answer.

"I didn't see much," he said. "When we got back to the lights, they were tipped over. All I saw was a tentacle or something drag it into the water. The Lieutenant freaked out and went to call the surface. That's when we found the divers waiting for the lift to return. The Marines were already on their way down. The divers must have called them already. What a mess. Two of the divers had to be flown out to McMurdo."

They sat there waiting for more, but Aaron had no more.

"What did this tentacle look like?" Agnet asked.

"It was like a giant octopus," he explained. "It drug the light fixture into the water before it stopped."

Dr. Knoll spoke up. "I helped the Medic bandage up one of the divers' legs. It looked like it was burned or scraped deeply."

"Possibly squeezed?" Agnet asked.

"Possibly," the doctor agreed.

"We have got to get to the bottom of this," Louise said.

For the next hour thoughts and hypotheses came flying out of the group. It's amazing how scientists can exaggerate the matters. Theories came in the form of anything from Sea beasts, Nazis, and Aliens. But nothing fit the bill.

"What was that thing?" asked Wade.

"Maybe it was an overgrown octopus caught in a closed environment. If that's the case there has to be more," Jason said.

"At least a breeding population," Dr. Knoll said.

Jason nodded his head in agreement.

"I'm going with the Nazis," Agnet said. "Those bastards ruled the world before World War 2. They explored this whole continent."

"That's absurd," Karen said. "The environment and geocology down there dated back at least 10,000 years, maybe more. I didn't see any evidence that the place was disturbed."

Louise was perplexed. She had brought back the rubbings from the stone ruins. She pulled them out of her pack and started to decipher them. Sylvia joined her as well as Dr. Knoll.

"This here is a name," Louise explained. "Hasfusute...," Louise read it out loud. "Here's another name, Gambaus...and here Xian Tian Sien. That is three different cultures. Egyptian, African, and Chinese. This is Mayan writing."

"Here, let me see," Jason said. He stared at the writing. He shifted the paper closer to his face. He looked at it until he finally came to a conclusion. "This is Enokian writing. I studied it the first year at college."

"What is Enokian?" Sylvia asked.

Louise chimed up and said, "The language of Enoch. It is said that the Angels use that language."

"The hell you say," Wade exclaimed.

"Precisely," Jason said. "The demons used it too."

"You're joking, right?" Wade asked.

"I'm afraid not," Louise said. "I've come across it before but just didn't know what it was. As a matter of fact, we saw this in California."

"Yes, we did see this before. On the inner door of the...," Sylvia started saying.

Louise interrupted her, "Nondisclosure, remember?"

Sylvia shut up and just nodded her head yes.

The doctor announced, "Now I would really like to know what happened in California."

"Nope," Louise said.

Karen just stayed quiet. Louise had told her what had happened and she wasn't going to get her friends in trouble.

"Be as it may," Sylvia said, "that doesn't explain the rotting mammoth. Or the wall."

Wade was pissed. He hated secrets. Especially government cover-ups. He thought about quitting right there on the spot. But the thought of missing out on a climatic discovery like this was unbearable. Now that he saw the cake, he wanted a piece of it. The survivalist finished eating and excused himself. He was going to talk to Lieutenant Groose. Maybe the Lieutenant could tell him more than the others. He found the spook in the radio room talking to McMurdo. He paused at the door to listen to the one-sided conversation.

"Yes…That's good to hear…Yes, sir, I understand…requesting troops to keep us safe then…excellent…Yes, sir, good to hear…0800 tomorrow then…excellent…out, sir." The Lieutenant put down the phone. "Aaron, glad you're here. Relay a message for me to the scientists. We will be having a briefing in one hour."

"Okay. Will we be going back down into the ice then?"

"Yes, we will," the Lieutenant answered him.

Aaron headed back to tell the scientists. He really didn't have much information, but he was going to at least tell them about the meeting so they could stop theorizing. Aaron really didn't like scientists. He found them to be annoying and snobby. Usually they got themselves and him into trouble all over the world. He had never lost a man on his trips and he didn't want to lose one now. Sylvia especially and also Louise. They had made this trip worthwhile and they didn't want to tie him down after the trip either. Yep, special girls. Mmmmm, mmmmm. He was looking forward to the way Sylvia sucked his cock and Louise's fucking technics… priceless. If only they would take him on together. Maybe….

Aaron returned to the commons area to find the whole group still sitting there and talking about the events of the day.

"Put yourselves at ease." he said loudly. "The Lieutenant wants you all here for a briefing in an hour."

"Great," the team said unanimously.

While he was there, he thought more about these two girls that had rocked his world. An hour passed and everyone gathered in the commons area waiting for the Lieutenant. He arrived after a few moments with another Lieutenant from the Marines.

"This is Lieutenant Winters. He will be heading our security detail while we are down in the ice. Okay, what you need to know," the Lieutenant continued. "The dive team encountered a creature about a hundred feet underwater that threatened to drag them to the bottom. They described this creature as a big octopus. They freed themselves and make it to the shore before the creature could reattach itself to them. Although the octopus did knock over the light tower and partly drag it into the lake, it did not try to go on land. So I think we can assume that it can't come on land. Therefore, my superiors have given me the go-ahead to explore the land around the lake. We will have extra Marines here tomorrow to watch the shoreline to make sure we are not bothered. Does that sound okay to you?"

Everyone agreed.

"Good. Then we will depart for the site at 0900 hours. The rest of the night is yours. Get some sleep and I'll see you in the morning."

The Marine Lieutenant stepped up next. "We have some rules for tomorrow.

- ➤ No going near the lake.
- ➤ Do not disturb the Marines. They need to keep watch.
- ➤ Don't get lost.

Anything happens and there is contact, make your way back to the lift immediately. Agreed?"

"Yes," everyone said.

"Okay. Then goodnight." he said and left the room.

The team returned to their rooms until supper. Each went over the events of the day. Dr. Knoll especially pondered what he had saw. Was there some kind of advanced race of humans that populated the Earth in the past? If there was, why did they die off? Why did they lose their technology? This was perplexing, he thought, until he thought of a major catastrophe. What if the Earth was plunged into an ice age so fast that no one had time to react? If the Earth crust shifted quickly that would explain the flash-frozen mammoth. Even the loss of technology. Forced back to the Ice Age, even an advanced society could lose most of their knowledge. They would revert back to a primitive race to survive. Maybe....

Karen met up with the doctor at suppertime. She was hooked in his charm. That catch he performed outside was the turning point of her life. She never had a man step so far out of his way to help her. He did it so innocently. He just didn't want to see her get hurt. Karen pondered a life with him after his crazy trip.

"Karen." He snapped his fingers in front of her face. "Earth to Karen."

"What? Sorry, I was just thinking," she answered with a smile.

"About what?"

"Oh, you know...stuff," she said with a shrug of her shoulders.

"Well, that is very descriptive."

They were eating goulash for supper that night. She went back into la-la land, when the doctor threw a noodle at her. It hit her in the face and fell to the table. What the....

"I guess I finally got your attention." he said with a big smile on his face.

Karen picked up the noodle and threw it back at him. She laughed as it hit his chest.

"Oh, that's funny." he said and laughed back. "Are you going to come by tonight?"

"Sure, I'll follow you from supper if that's okay?"

"Absolutely," he answered. "I have a movie we can watch on my laptop if you like?"

"That would be good," Karen said.

"Great."

They hurried through supper and headed off to the doctor's room. Karen sat next to Charles and they got pretty cozy as they watched the file on the doctor's laptop. They enjoyed each other's company and she found excuses to kiss him. She reached up and kissed his cheek in the middle of the movie, so he kissed her back on the lips. She laid down on the couch and he laid down on top of her. Next thing you know, they weren't watching the movie anymore. Karen pulled off his shirt and kissed his chest. She helped him take off her own shirt and bra. He laid down again with his lips upon her tits. He squeezed one tit while he sucked on the other tit.

"Ahhh," she moaned as he circled her nipple with his tongue.

He moved down and kissed her across her tummy and especially around her belly button.

"Ohhh," she moaned.

He unbuttoned her pants and slid them off. He kissed her waist and pulled off her panties. Karen moaned as he kissed his way down to her clit. He flicked his tongue on her button, making Karen scream.

"Oh, yes."

He sucked really hard and then flicked his tongue against her button, before sucking real hard again. Throwing Karen into a full-on come. She pulled him up for a kiss. Karen tasted her own pussy juice on his lips and loved it.

"My turn," Karen whispered as she helped him lay down.

Karen unzipped his pants and pulled both pants and boxers down and off him. She kissed him on the chest and moved down to his hard, long cock. He clenched in anticipation as she kissed her way down the side of his cock and went to his ball sack. She stroked his cock as she sucked on his balls. She popped them in and out of her mouth and then sucked hard on his sack. He moaned in ecstasy as she pushed his cock deep into her mouth.

She paused briefly to say, "Watch this. I learned this from Sylvia."

She took him deep inside her throat all the way until her lips touched his balls. She licked his balls each time her lips touched them. Just before she licked his balls, Karen would hold still and moan. The vibrations from her moan would be felt from the tip of his cock to his balls.

"Oh, God," he moaned as his come came spurting out of his cock and down Karen's throat.

When his come hit the back of Karen's throat, she swallowed every bit of it. Karen wiped her mouth and he helped her to bed. Karen got on all fours and he took her from behind. Like an animal, he drove his cock deep inside her and rammed her fast and hard.

"Ohhhh....Aaaaa...," he grunted over and over as he fucked her deep, hard, and fast.

Karen screamed as he fucked her. "Ohhhh...Oh, God, baby. Ohhhh."

Her moaning wasn't stopping and he knew she was close to coming. So he pushed his cock in her as hard as he could and she let out a scream as she came.

"Oh, baby. Yesss." She looked back at him with approval in her eyes and a smile on her face. Then she realized something. "No come?"

"Not yet," he said.

"Okay," she said back. "You know what that means."

She reached for some lube. His smile got bigger as he realized what she was doing. She lubed up his cock a bit and then laid on her stomach. The doctor was in heaven when the tip of his cock entered her hot asshole. He slowly worked the rest of his cock in inch by inch, enjoying the sensation. When he had it all in her hole, he slowly started to pump in her and out of her.

She moaned and didn't stop moaning the whole time he was in her. "Oh, baby....Oh, God," she was saying as he slowly fucked her up the butt. Her ass was tight and hot around his dick and Karen moaned loudly as he pushed it deep into her little butthole.

"Ohhhh, God, baby....Ohhh," Karen cried out as he plunged it in and out of her ass.

Like before, he hugged her and held her tits with both hands as he rammed her slow but hard.

"Oh, yeah," she went on.

He felt his dick get ready to shoot his load and he groaned as he came up her ass. "Oh, Goddd."

They laid there in the moment just soaking in all the pleasure they both just had. Eventually, he got off her and she cuddled up beside him and fell asleep. In the morning, they both hit the showers and then headed to breakfast with plenty of contentment. Everyone was in a hurry to get back to the site, so they ate in a hurry. They all huddled together at the lift waiting to go down into the hole. A platoon of Marines went down first to secure the beach. Next went Lieutenant Groose and the Lieutenant Winters with a load of digging equipment that Louise insisted on having. The crew was the last to go down and they went down in groups of four.

Chapter 5

At the bottom we all assembled before we went our separate ways. Karen and I headed towards the mammoth. Louise and Sylvia went towards the stone markers. Wade and Aaron headed down the beach looking for signs of declimatization. Agnet and Jason went looking for vegetation.

Karen reached the mammoth first and stayed back well away from the smell. "What are we here for?"

"Well, we are not going to dig up that animal, if that's what you're asking."

"Then why are we here?" Karen asked him again.

"You see the section on the back of the mammoth? That colored patch there?"

"Yes. What is it?" Karen asked him.

"I think it might be a harness."

"What?" she asked, making sure she heard him right.

"I'm pretty sure that is part of a harness used to haul stuff or use the animal for labor. Which means humans were using mammoths for manual labor. If we find out for sure...."

He pulled on the strap, trying to yank it from under the belly of the freeze-dried mammoth. He tugged a little harder. The strap popped out from under the great beast.

"See…."

"See what?" Karen asked.

"It's a belt buckle."

Sure enough, it was a four-inch belt buckle made out of bronze.

"This piece alone proves that man was advanced enough to smith bronze in the Ice Age. Well, before the so-called Bronze Age."

"That's very interesting," Karen said.

"Yes, it is," I said back. "That means the timeline of man is way off by thousands of years. I'm going to find by how much."

She stared at me as I pondered what to do.

"Let's go see what your two friends are up to," I said as we started to leave.

"With pleasure," Karen said with relief as she held her nose from the stink.

We came upon Louise and Sylvia digging by the first stone marker. They were digging in a circle grid around the stone.

"Do you need some help?" Charles asked as they jumped into the hole.

"Sure," Louise said as she handed us both a shovel.

I went immediately to the front of the stone where the engravings were. They kind of looked like graves to me, so I wanted to start in the front. I dug carefully until I saw a bone. It was a femur bone from a human.

"Louise!" I yelled. "Come here. I found something."

Karen stood next to me staring at the bone sticking out of the dirt.

"It's a femur bone," Louise said as she knelt down to look at it.

In no time at all, we had a whole skeleton laid out in front of us.

"So, this is a graveyard," Louise said. "Let's start in front of each stone and see if we are right."

I'm not a morbid man, but it was kind of fun digging up graves. The second skeleton was wearing silk. So, we thought it was Chinese. The third was wearing a necklace of gold. The fourth had a Mayan headdress buried with it. The fifth was an Israelite. We figured that out by the signet ring he was wearing. When we dug up the sixth body, everyone stood back and stared. It had an elongated skull. Not unusual to find in Egypt or South

America. Hell, some were even found in Europe. But in Antarctica, this was a first. The skeleton looked normal other than its head was three inches taller than a normal human.

We went to the seventh grave wondering what we would find. There under the dirt was a red-bearded mummy. Fully dried skin on the body. It was also at least eight feet tall. Its teeth had protruded out of its mouth because of the drying process. He had all the cuts in the right places so we know he was mummified like the Egyptians. But long red hair and a red beard? He was also wearing what looked like cotton.

"What the hell did we find?" asked Louise.

"This doesn't make any kind of sense," said Sylvia.

Karen stood in awe of the find.

"I'm shocked," I said. "Cotton wasn't used in Egypt until at least the 2nd-Century B.C."

"Yes. This is too early of a time period for that," Louise said.

"What?" Karen asked in confusion.

"If we're assuming that we had subjects from 10,000 years ago or more, that means it's way too early for cotton clothing. They should be wearing furs," I told her.

I stood there shaking my head in wonder. I couldn't figure out this new timeline we had going.

"Doctor," Louise interrupted his thoughts. "Let's get some samples to test back in the lab."

"Oh, yes, of course," Dr. Knoll said as he snapped out of his thoughts.

He started to take core samples of each individuals bone marrow in hopes of finding DNA. Next, they moved onto the mammoth and took samples from its teeth and tusks. The doctor showed the harness to Louise and Sylvia. Louise thought that it could be for pulling huge stones. She cut off a piece of the strap for carbon dating. Agnet and Jason joined them at the mammoth site with some wood samples, and they even brought back some rocks for Karen to study. Jason found more green patches of vegetation and brought back some samples to examine.

"Okay, folks, it's time to head back," said Lieutenant Groose.

Lieutenant Groose directed them back to the lift. The Marines surrounded them as they were lifted up to the top. The doctor was on the last lift up. When it reached the ice tunnel, he saw the Marines go running to the lake. One was shooting at something on the shore. The lift entered the ice tunnel and the show was over.

Back at the base he asked, "What happened?"

"Just war nerves. One man thought he saw the octopus in the shallow water or something."

The scientists went to work as soon as they came back. Dr. Knoll took a bit of all the samples and started carbon dating. He wanted to know how old these samples were. He only showed up at supper to grab a tray and took his food with him to go back to his workstation. Karen came by and sat down next to him.

"I studied the rock Jason brought back, and they are glacial rocks. So they were subjected to some amount of ice dragging across them," Karen stated.

"I got the first set of carbon tests done." He smiled and danced with excitement. "The mammoth tests back to 12,500 years old and the strap is the same date. The Chinese and Egyptian body is 10,000 years old. I'm still waiting on the others. Ah, here they come."

An email was sent to his laptop from McMurdo.

"The Israelite and Mayan bodies tested at 11,000 years. This is when it gets weird," he said. "The elongated skull tests at 14,000 years old. The redhaired, bearded skeleton tests the same. Now the person we tested for DNA strands. Karen, I think you need to brace yourself for this one."

"What is it, Charles?" she asked, sitting on the edge of her seat.

"This guy was from Western Europe. His closest match is the Sulutreans or Clovis people. We are still waiting on the DNA from the elongated subject. Just think of it, Euorapoid hunters down here in Antarctica."

"We need to tell Louise," Karen said with excitement.

She dashed out of the room with the doctor hot on her heels. Louise was surprised by the dates and DNA tests.

"Well, Clovis bodies have been showing up around the United States that predates any of the Native American tribes known to live there. Maybe they were all over the globe. There were even graves found as far away as China. What about the rest?" Louise asks.

"We are still waiting on the test results," Dr. Knoll answered. "But I'm mostly interested in that elongated skull fellow."

"Yes, that DNA should turn out to be interesting," Louise stated.

"Hopefully we will get those results before tomorrow's return to the caverns," said the doctor.

Karen was holding on to the doctor's arm and Louise knew what she was after, so she excused herself and headed towards her room. On the way back to the lab, Karen and Charles flirted and made small talk through the corridors. By the time they got back to the lab, they were making out against the wall. It started with kissing and continued on with them caressing each other. They shot past the lab and headed towards Karen's room, where they stayed the rest of the night.

In the morning after everyone ate breakfast, they all loaded into the snow cats to proceed to the site. Karen was still holding on to the doctor's arm. Sylvia noticed how Karen was hanging on to the doctor.

She whispered to Louise, "Oh, yeah, she's doomed."

Louise laughed and said, "Maybe it will be you next time."

"Oh, no," Sylvia said and shook her head. "I'm not going down that road ever again."

"Yeah, we'll see." Louise laughed.

They all headed down the hole speedily so they wouldn't waste any part of the day. When the Scientists all got down there, they were surrounded by confused Marines.

"What is it?" asked Jason.

"We found something on this morning's security sweep that we think you all need to see."

The Marines surrounded the group of Scientists and led them down the beach. They went farther down the beach than any one of them had ever gone. They went so far until they came upon the rest of the Marines guarding a pile of equipment stacked on the upper beach.

Now I didn't freak out over finding equipment down there. It wasn't even the World War 2 guns that did it. Nor was it the crates themselves, but what was on them that made everyone's jaw drop. There plain as day was a stamped Swastika and the letters SS under it. I gulped in a breath as the group just stood there surrounding the pile of equipment. No one spoke for a moment or two.

Then one of the Marines yelled from the beach, "I found a body down here."

We all headed towards the beach and stared at the dead body of a long-dead SS Storm Trooper laying on the beach. Inside his uniform was nothing but a skeleton. His face was mummified by time and skin protruded into the holes where his eyes would have been. Around one of his legs was a shriveled-up giant arm of the octopus creature that ran back into the water. His gun was pointing into the water, obviously trying to get away from the creature in the lake. The tentacle was wound around his leg very tightly. Tight enough to tear the skin and muscle right off the bone.

"The creature had ripped off all his skin and flesh down to the bone," said the Biologist, Jason.

There beside the body was a pill bottle. Jason picked it up and smelled the contents.

"It's cyanide." he said as he put the bottle back down on the soldier's uniform.

"He must have killed himself after the injury," said one of the Marines.

Dr. Knoll went to the water's edge to see if there was anything more to the tentacle. After so many years, there was nothing left after the water line. He stopped to look deeper into the water and then returned to the group. As he was going back, Jason was taking samples from the creature and the soldier.

"That's a good idea. I'll need some of those later," said the doctor.

Jason nodded that he understood.

Karen returned to the doctor's side. "Is that what I think it is?" she asked.

"Yep. That's a Nazi." he said as they stared at the dead soldier.

"How did it get here?" Louise asked in bewilderment.

"Well," Lieutenant Groose spoke up, "there was always legends that the Nazis had a hidden base down here. Maybe part of that story was true. May I remind you all of your nondisclosure agreements. Not a word of this outside of the camp or base, besides, who would believe it, anyway? Sylvia, since you are the only Historian here, I would like you and your partner to stay and catalog the artifacts. The rest of you are free to go back to the other sites."

Louise asked the doctor, "Could you stay with Sylvia so I can go back to the other dig site?"

The doctor agreed. Karen went back with Louise instead. The doctor had agreed for one reason only. He was fascinated by the fact that Nazis were down here in Antarctica. He studied the pile of cargo and equipment carefully. Sylvia was categorizing the items as the doctor was pulling them out.

"Notice something, Doctor?" Sylvia asked him.

"Yes, if you're referring to there being five of each item. Especially gas masks and cold winter gear. I would say there was five soldiers here."

"Yes, that's what I figure too," Sylvia said in agreement.

"So, where are the rest of the bodies?" the doctor asked.

"Maybe the lake creature got them," Sylvia answered.

Jason and Agnet were studying the body down by the lake, when one of the Marines yelled for them down the beach a few hundred yards. Sylvia and the doctor took off running as well as Jason and Agnet, to find out what was happening. There laying a few yards into the water was another skeleton wearing a Nazi uniform.

A Marine went into the water to retrieve the body and he didn't come out…the octopus creature grabbed his leg and pulled him under. Two other Marines started to go in and help him, but they were too late. The first Marine was gone. Dr. Knoll and Sylvia made it there just in time to see him go under. The last Marine radioed it in and Lieutenant Groose forbade anyone from entering the water. He came running up with more Marines in an attempt to find the missing man. But it was too late…he was gone for good.

"That's it. I want everyone away from the shore at least ten meters," Lieutenant Groose yelled as he waved everyone back.

Sylvia and Dr. Knoll went back to inventorying the Nazi cargo. They were followed by Jason and Agnet.

"Well, that was something," Jason said to the group.

"Poor man," Sylvia said.

"At least we know what happened to the other German soldiers," the doctor said.

Agnet agreed. They finished up and the Marines took the cargo away. The group went to meet up with Karen and Louise. They were at the graveyard digging again. Louise was sitting waist deep in a hole as they approached. Karen was kneeling beside her with a puzzled look on her face.

"Oh, boy. What is it now?" Sylvia asked them.

Louise pulled out a small shiny object and started to clean the dirt off of it.

"What is it?" Sylvia asked as she finally got a good look at the object.

"I'm pretty sure it's a gold cross," Louise said and picked up another small piece and put them together. "Yep, it's a cross."

"Keep digging. Maybe we will find another body," Sylvia said.

"I'm digging as fast as I can," Louise said and she handed Sylvia a small shovel. "Here, help."

Sylvia jumped into the hole and started digging. They dug down a little bit farther and found some bones. Then an old Navy uniform, and then a whole Navy sailor.

He had a notice in his chest pocket and it read:

OPERATION: High Jump
TOP SECRET

"This man is from 1947. He must have been part of Admiral Bird's expedition," Sylvia said with awe.

They were about to take samples from the sailor, when they heard a gruff voice from behind them.

"What the hell are you doing here? Why are you digging up my father's grave?"

A man came out of the shadows wearing an old Army sweater and a uniform with a flat hat on.

"We're here on an exploratory expedition," said Dr. Knoll.

"Who's in charge of this expedition?" the new man asked.

"That would be Lieutenant Groose," said Louise.

"Here he comes right now," Jason said, and the Lieutenant came up and introduced himself.

"Where did you come from?" the stranger asked.

"We came down an ice tunnel that we drilled in the ceiling over there." The Lieutenant pointed at the lift area. "Who are you and how did you get down here?"

"I'm Henry Wiseman and I've lived down here my whole life." He motioned back at the shadows. "This is my wife, Ingred."

A small blonde woman came shyly out of the shadows. She was holding a German Mouser machine gun at her side.

"How did you survive down here?" Jason asked curiously.

"Oh, we have a village around the bend of the lake over there." Henry pointed to the left of the shore. "Would you like to meet the others?" he asked in earnest.

"Sure," the Lieutenant said as he directed the few Marines he had with him to follow them.

He sent one Marine back to tell the others where they were going. Then they all followed the Arctic strangers to their village. They walked for about ten minutes and stopped in amazement at what they saw. It was a giant Pyramid halfway into ruins.

Sylvia pointed up and whispered, "Louise, look."

"Yes, I see," Louise whispered back.

By the looks of its state, it had been under a glacier for a thousand years or more. There was no rough edges to the structure. As if it had been shaved smooth by shifting ice. At the top was a torch lit and shining shadows above it upon the ice ceiling. From its inner chamber near the top came a man dressed in an old Russian uniform.

"Everyone, come meet the strangers," Henry yelled out.

Out of the shadows around the Pyramid came several men, women, and children. The children came running up to the expedition team and started touching them. It was like they couldn't believe they were real. Louise swooped down to pick up the youngest child, who was beckoning to be picked up.

"Here you go, honey," Louise said as she handed the little girl a power bar. She handed out more to the children around her. "Sylvia, is there more in the pack?"

"Yes," said Sylvia as she pulled out a full box of bars.

They both started handing them out at this point so no one was left out. One of the adult females came up wearing an Australian Army uniform.

"Where did you all come from?" she asked.

"We dug a tunnel through the ice," Dr. Knoll told her.

"Well, we are glad for that." She added, "We were just about out of food and medical supplies. Oh, how rude of me. I'm Nurse Kathy Barns of the Australian Army."

They all introduced themselves in turn. Nurse Barns was a tall, slender woman in her 50s. She had blonde hair with a slight grey tint. She looked a little malnutrition but otherwise in good health.

"How long have you been down here?" Dr. Knoll asked her.

"I've been here since 1975. I and a few others were on an expedition into some under glacier caverns that formed on a very hot summer. We made it here after the entrance to the ice cavern collapsed. Took us two weeks of going through maze-like caverns under the glacier ice till we found this place. When we got here, we found all these survivors living around the lake. We have sent out teams to try to find our way to the surface...but we have yet to find any sort of access," she explained in her thick Australian accent.

"What do you eat down here?" Jason asked.

"We fish and grow our own potatoes as well as a few other vegetables. Sometimes, we find lost supplies from other lost expeditions in the ice caves."

"How many of you are there?" Lieutenant Groose asked.

"Our numbers are 50," said Henry.

"I'll radio the supplies to be dropped immediately," said the Lieutenant.

He stepped aside and started radioing the other Marines back at the lift. Within a half an hour, there was Navy personnel all over the small village rendering aid to the inhabitants. They set up a medical tent in the middle of the village that was assessing everyone's health. Nurse Kathy was a big help in registering the patients and administering shots and food rations.

Karen stepped up to Dr. Knoll at one point and asked, "Are these people willing to return to the surface?"

"I was hoping they all would," he answered. "Lieutenant Groose is prepping them to leave."

"But what if some of them want to stay? I wouldn't want to be separated from what I called home for so many years."

"I'm sure they will give them the choice," said the doctor.

Karen wasn't sure. She went to talk to Sylvia and Louise about the matter. Louise reassured her that she would take up the matter with Lieutenant Groose when the time came.

"But for now, they have to be immunized and treated for malnutrition before they could be moved anywhere," Louise told Karen.

More tents were brought down and placed around the village. The Scientists were going to stay with the villagers for the time being. They all went about in their own science fields, studying what they could given this time period. Sylvia and Jason stayed mostly in the village studying and learning the culture. Listening to stories of this ragtag bunch of people. They spoke with the oldest member of the village, an Englishman named Edwin Toholms, who had been there since the 1950s.

He told them of how some warm years, the ceiling of the cavern would melt open and let in more light. The ground would sprout up green and plentiful. Then other years where they would almost starve from the lack of light. If it wasn't for the abundant of fish in the lake, they all would have died.

"This year we have not fished because of the beast," Mr. Toholms said.

"How many octopuses are there in the lake?" Jason asked.

"Not sure," Mr. Toholms answered. "Usually only one or two. But there is always smaller ones that are in the process of growing into monsters. The little ones don't hunt you as long as you stay close to shore. But the big ones, they can drag you under, never to be seen again."

In the village everyone was cooperating with the Navy personnel. Mostly they were glad to get medical treatment and food, of course. But one group didn't step forward for help. A band of five older Russians refused to be seen. They stayed mostly in the Pyramid by themselves, not participating in any of the rescue efforts. They refused the food as well. A translator was sent down from the nearby Russian camp by Lake Vostok to help in their aid. The translator asked for the help of Nurse Kathy and Jason, to go with him and help speak to the Russians.

"Oh," Lieutenant Groose said as the group was leaving. "Please remind them that the Cold War is over."

"Will do," the translator said.

After the translator explained the situation in the world nowadays and what the soldiers have missed in the last 40 years, the Russian men seemed to calm down about the situation and accepted the aid that was being given. But they made it perfectly clear that they weren't going anywhere. This put Lieutenant Groose on the spot. He had to return to the topside and connect with the Admiral at McMurdo to see what he wanted him to do. This would take a few more days till his return. After he left everyone was waiting for his return when…

Dr. Knoll and Karen were enjoying their night off in the camp. They took a walk down by the beach after supper and were about to return to the village, when there was a big explosion. They ran to the village to see what had happened. Sylvia was laying on the ground in front of the Pyramid motionless. One of her legs was badly damaged in the explosion.

The steps of the Pyramid were burned and a couple of them were crumbled. The villagers were scrambling to put out some fires that had spread by the explosion. Dr. Knoll and Karen could not see the rest of their colleges anywhere. They asked a Marine standing guard by the village what happened, and he motioned for them to get under cover.

"We can't leave her here," Karen said with fear in her voice.

"No, we can't," the doctor said and picked her up and carried her back to the village.

They rushed her past the makeshift barricade that's manned by a Marine, just before a bullet whizzed by the doctor and hit the wooden fence.

"That was close," Karen said as they continued to the other side of the village to the medical tent.

When they got there, there was five to ten villagers hurt and getting medical help. In one of the last cots they put Sylvia down. The field Medic came over and pushed them aside with Nurse Kathy by his side, and started to treat her.

"What happened?" Karen asked them.

"We don't know," the Medic told her. "The wounded just keep coming in."

"Let's find out what happened," Dr. Knoll said to Karen.

They headed back towards the Pyramid and slowly,carefully made their way through the village commotion. When they hit the fence, they stayed low until they got to the Marines grouped behind the fence. They had taken up a defensive position.

The Marine Sergeant looked at them and said, "You civilians need to get back."

"We are looking for our friends," the doctor explained. "What happened here?"

"The Russians are held up in the Pyramid. They have hostages. They set off some kind of explosion, to detour us from saving them, sir."

"Why?" Karen asked in confusion.

"There was an argument about leaving, ma'am. That's all I know."

"Is Louise up there?" Karen asked.

"There's two women and two men in their custody," said the Sergeant.

"Oh, God," Karen whispered with fear.

The doctor and Karen moved back off the line, out of range of the fire. 762x54 shells make a loud pop as they go off. It was used in the Mosin-Nagant World War, a sniper rifle and it packs enough punch to reach out a thousand yards. The rounds, once ignited, fly straight and whiz by without tumbling in the slightest. The bullets slam up against their target with enough force to knock it clean over. Those were the bullets that was flying through the village. One hit the stone wall next to the doctor and Karen. It dug deep into the rock.

"That was too close," Dr. Knoll said as he motioned for Karen to move back. "We need to get to some place safer."

Inside the Pyramid Chamber, Jason and the translator were tied up and sitting up against the cold stone wall. Next to them, Louise was laying after suffering damage from the explosion on her arm and her head. Agnet was tying a bandage around Louise's head. Louise was limp from the shockwave and Agnet tried to help her by keeping her warm, with her jacket and by using her body heat.

It's funny, Agnet had never taken the time to get to know Louise, but now she was holding her like a baby in her arms. At least she was warm, her pulse is good, so I think she just passed out, Agnet thought, I hope. Agnet held her tight waiting for a sign of life from Louise. She pulled Louise up onto her lap and moved her head down to Louise's face. She kissed Louise's forehead slightly and then used her cheek to see if Louise was breathing strongly. Yep, she is breathing, Agnet thought. I just need to keep her warm. She looked at the Russians at the entrance to the chamber, they all had guns. Then, she looked at the two men sitting up against the wall next to them. They were tied, hands and feet together with gags in both of their mouths.

She felt helpless sitting there with Louise in her lap. She applied pressure to Louise's cut on her arm and tried to bandage it with a piece of cloth she ripped off her shirt. The bleeding had stopped after about two to three winds of the cloth. She checked for any other cuts that might be bleeding and found none. Then she checked herself. One of her ankles was swollen and not moving. Agnet swung it to her side to look at it. It was black and blue and swollen to about double its size. She could hear the Russians talking in their foreign language. It sounded like they were arguing.

Outside one of the Marines yelled out to them, "Come out and give yourselves up!!!"

They argued some more, then shot at the Marines. Agnet shuttered a bit as she thought of dying. She made up her mind to protect this lady, herself, and the guys. She put Louise down gently and slowly, carefully made her way to the translator. She pulled out the gag in his mouth. She united his hands and snuck back to Louise.

The translator united his feet and then untied Jason's hands. He went back to sitting so the Russians would not know he was united. As soon as Jason was united, they started to sneak up on the Russians. Jason grabbed one of the guns that the soldier was holding and wrestled it away from him. The translator did the same and the other three Russians ran as Jason and the translator shot at them. They ran out of the Pyramid and were shot by the Marines. The other two that were still in the Pyramid chamber were pushed to the ground and tied up.

"All clear," Jason yelled out as he went through the entrance.

"Clear," the Marines echoed.

They took the two Russians and headed out of the chamber. Jason and the translator grabbed Louise and got her out of the Pyramid. The Medic and Dr. Knoll put her on a stretcher and headed back to the med tent. Agnet followed as best she could until the Marines put her on a stretcher and carried her the rest of the way. As she was transferred to a cot, she passed out from the stress and the pain of her ankle.

Dr. Knoll helped move Louise to the medical tent. Then he helped move Agnet to the other cot. She passed out shortly after. He was at a loss for words. What had gone wrong? He was just enjoying a peaceful night with Karen and then all hell broke loose. He looked around. Where was Karen? He ran out of the tent and looked around. She wasn't there.

"Karen!!! Karen!!!" he yelled. "Has anyone seen Karen?"

No one had seen her. He went back to their tent and pulled open the door. Karen wasn't there. He went back to the Pyramid and she wasn't there either. He went back to the last place he had seen her and looked behind the fence. There she was sitting up against the wall. She was holding her side.

"What's wrong?" he asked.

"I got shot," she said.

He picked her up and carried her to the med tent. He placed her on a cot and yelled, "Medic in need….I need a Medic over here."

The Medic ran over and looked at the patient. "Let me see." he said as he pulled away the cloth bandage.

There about an inch on her side was a bleeding hole. He sat her up and looked at the other side.

"Okay," the Medic said and laid her down on a bandage. Then he covered up the hole on the front. "It's a through and through. She'll be okay. I want you to watch her. I'll get her in to get stitched up soon," the Medic said to the doctor.

The doctor sat by her side and held her hand. "You'll be okay." he said and squeezed her hand.

She looked back at him as he held her hand. She was so happy to be there with him. He had found and saved her again. She loved him and that was that.

Sylvia was awake and in a lot of pain. Her leg had been cut by some shrapnel from the explosion. Her lower leg had been bandaged up and she was on a saline drip. She couldn't move much, nor did she want to. She saw Louise and Agnet on the other side of the tent. Louise had a bandage on her arm and a bandage on her head. She was not awake nor was Agnet. Outside she could see the Medic stitching up Karen.

"What's going on?" she asked, almost screaming.

Nurse Kathy came over to calm her down. "It's alright. Everyone is okay. You are suffering from shock and from the blast. It will pass." She sat down next to Sylvia and held her hand.

"Louise, is she...?" Sylvia couldn't finish her sentence. She was afraid of the answer.

"No, she is fine," Kathy said.

"Good, and Agnet?"

"She is fine too. She just sprained her ankle and bumped her head."

"Good. I hope everyone else is okay."

"Well, we did have some casualties with the Russians," stated Kathy. "Three got shot after taking hostages. The Marines didn't have a choice. They wouldn't give up."

"Oh," exclaimed Sylvia.

She then laid back down exhausted. Karen got stitched up and was laying on the cot trying to get her strength back. Dr. Knoll stayed with her the whole time. He held her hand through the whole experience. He was so sorry for leaving her behind at the fence.

"I will never leave you again," he promised her.

She nodded her head yes that she understood. Karen smiled at him, her big hero. Agnet woke up next, her ankle was still swollen but some of the color was gone. The Medic determined that it wasn't broken and that she would be fine after a week. Louise woke with a big headache and was told what had happened. She was very pleased to hear that Agnet had saved them and taken care of her. Louise was intrigued by this Greek beauty.

"Agnet," she called out.

"Yes?" Agnet answered.

"Thank you for saving my life."

"Oh, it was nothing," Agnet said. "You would have done the same thing."

"Still. Can I at least take you out to dinner and drinks?" Louise asked.

"Sure," she agreed with a sheepish smile.

A few days later the team was back at the base. Agnet was up on crutches, and Louise was feeling better. So they decided to catch that dinner. They sat with Karen and Dr. Knoll at supper. They all talked about what had happened and what they think was going to happen. Karen decided to head home with Dr. Knoll after the expedition was over. He was going to help her get a job at the University of Michigan and an apartment near his own.

Louise laughed and said, "It would be cheaper if you moved in together."

Karen smiled and looked at Charles.

"Well," he said, "I do have a big place, maybe you would be more comfortable staying with me."

She smiled and said, "I would love to move in with you."

He smiled back at her and said, "Good, then that's what we'll do."

Karen and Charles left the other two and headed for their room. Louise and Agnet talked all through the rest of the meal. Agnet loved the way Louise stared at her. Louise loved looking at her beautiful eyes. At one point through the meal, Louise reached over the table and grabbed Agnet's hands. It sent a fire through both of the girls. They helped each other to Louise's room for after-dinner drinks. Agnet could barely stand on her sprained ankle, so Louise helped her sit on the bed. Louise poured them a mixed drink and sat down next to Agnet, and turned on her mp3 player. "Levitate" by Imagine Dragons was playing.

"The light in your eyes... You're my shooting star

I'm flying high above...."

The song went on as they stared at each other's eyes.

After Louise finished her drink, and she put her glass down and leaned in for a kiss as the song repeated, "Just levitate... Just levitate... Just levitate," over and over again. Agnet kissed her back with passion and longing. She reached down and touched Louise's tits, caressing them through her thin blouse.

"Ahh." Louise paused her kissing to breathe out with a moan.

Louise grabbed Agnet's tits with her hands and pulled them out of her shirt. She started kissing and licking them. Agnet groaned as she laid down on the bed. Louise followed her down, sucking on her nipples one after other. Agnet held Louise's head as she kissed her breasts. Louise stopped for a second to remove her shirt and bra, while Agnet did the same.

"Ahh." It was Agnet's turn to moan out as Louise kissed down from her neck to her tits, and slowly kissed her way down to her pants. Louise unbuttoned and pulled off her pants and panties and let them fall to the floor. Louise went in for the kill and licked her button.

"Ohhh," Agnet groaned as Louise licked harder. "Ohhhh, owww," Agnet yelled as Louise bit her clit and licked the sting of pain away.

Agnet shivered and came as Louise shoved her tongue deep inside Agnet's wet pussy. She shuddered to a stop as Louise finally let go of Agnet's clit with her teeth.

"Ohh, that was amazing," she said with a well-pleasured look on her face. "Okay, now it's my turn."

Agnet and Louise switched places. Agnet started with Louise's huge tits. She caressed them with her hands and kissed each nipple. She rubbed her tongue around Louise's hard nipples and lightly bit them.

Louise screamed in ecstasy, "Ohhh, God."

Agnet moved down Louise's stomach and kissed her belly button. Then she licked her way down to Louise's waiting clit. She rubbed her clit with her tongue and stuck two of her fingers into Louise's wet pussy. She poked in and out as she licked and kissed her button.

"Ooohhhh," cried Louise. "Oh, God." Louise came hard to the movement of Agnet's fingers. "That was awesome. But I have more."

"What?" Agnet asked.

Louise pulled out a double dildo.

"Ohhh," Agnet exclaimed with a big smile.

Louise put one side of the dildo into Agnet's pussy, slowly inch by inch until it was in her all the way. Then she jumped on top of her and sat on the other side. Louise leaned back, so they were facing away from each other, and started to push back and forth.

"Ohhh…mmmm….yessss."

They both moaned until they both came together.

Louise put away the dildo and they laid together, exhausted and in bliss for the night.

The next morning, the villagers were extracted from the ice cavern and introduced into the base community. All of them decided to leave, but many decided to stay in Antarctica as advisors. They were to lead expeditions down into the ice caves and helped scientists get their bearings. Sylvia and Louise chose to stay for a while to do more studies on the Pyramid. That could have had something to do with Agnet staying. Karen and Dr. Knoll left to start a new adventure in Michigan. The Survivalist stayed on while Wade went home right after the cemetery was found.

A month later back in Michigan, Dr. Knoll was helping Karen move into his house. He paused for a second to think of all the stuff he encountered in Antarctica. Karen came into the room and put down her box of dishes and kissed him on the cheek.

"Yep, that certainly was some trip." he said as he followed her to the bedroom.

She pulled off her shirt and threw it back at him. He turned at the last step into the bedroom and said, "Yep, some trip."